PIERO VENTURA

COMMUNICATION

Means and Technologies for Exchanging Information

With the Collaboration of
Max Casalini

Laura Battaglia
Pierluigi Longo
Massimo Messina

HOUGHTON MIFFLIN COMPANY
BOSTON 1994

CONTENTS

Copyright © 1993 by Arnoldo Mondadori Editore S.p.A.
English translation © 1994 by Arnoldo Mondadori
Editore S.p.A.
First American edition 1994
Originally published in Italy in 1993 by Mondadori
All rights reserved. For information about permission to
reproduce selections from this book, write to Permissions,
Houghton Mifflin Company, 215 Park Avenue South,
New York, New York 10003.
Printed in Spain by Artes Gráficas Toledo, S.A.
10 9 8 7 6 5 4 3 2 1
D.L.TO:383-1994

Library of Congress Cataloging-in-Publication Data
Ventura, Piero.
  [Communicazione. English]
  Communication : means and technologies for exchanging information /
Piero Ventura ; with the collaboration of Max Casalini . . . [et al.].
    p. cm.
  ISBN 0-395-66789-5
  1. Communication—History—Juvenile literature.
  [1. Communication—History.] I. Casalini, Max. II. Title
P91.2.V4613 1994
302.2' 09—dc20   94-4521
                                                            CIP
                                                            AC

INTRODUCTION

Everybody wants to communicate, and people everywhere talk about ways of communicating. *Communication* is one of the words we hear most often, but do we really know what it means?

To communicate means to transfer thoughts and messages from one place to another or from one individual to another. The subject of communication is enormous, and this book was designed to present a panorama of the history of communication from a chronological point of view, showing how communication was born and how it evolved with changing needs.

Following the evolution of communication means taking a trip that begins in earliest history. People left traces of their existence with a great quantity of signs and symbols, on carved tablets of clay and ivory and on monuments. They left messages, described events, and handed down customs. The use of parchment and pen and ink was only one stage in the evolution of the exchange of information, which then led to printing, typewriters, and, today, the computer.

Communication is also the telling and retelling of stories, legends, events. Important moments in the social life of each epoch have traditionally been handed down orally, by singers and musicians performing in the open, and in theaters, by actors in comedies and tragedies. Today the theater enables us to express ideas and emotions, to send messages, or to make known existential suffering or the desire for change.

Art is a form of communication that relates ideas through painting and sculpture.

The arrival of the camera has made it possible to immortalize moments of real life; films and television create dreams and give birth to hope. Information has the capacity to affect our thoughts and our actions. Communication is indispensable to knowing and to being known, to learning about the past, to confronting the present and predicting the future, to growing through the exchange of information, and above all to understanding that we are not alone.

HIEROGLYPHICS

The ancient Greeks are credited with inventing many aspects of modern civilization: Euclid invented geometry; Socrates, philosophy; and Aeschylus, tragedy. But they knew that none of these inventions would have been possible without the written word, and credit for that invention goes to the ancient Egyptians, who had been using writing thousands of years before the Greek civilization began.

The oldest known examples of writing are clan markings on vases. Later, writing in hieroglyphics, giving the names of people or groups of people, appeared on stone tablets and ivory. Later still came brief phrases, prayers to the gods, and records of the building of monuments. There was still not a lot of writing around, but a small flame had been kindled and was beginning to spread its light. Writing was now able to record facts and express ideas. During the XII dynasty, under the influence of learned men, written language developed quickly.

The Egyptians wrote in hieroglyphics, stylized pictures that are also called pictographs or ideograms. Each picture meant not only what it looked like but also the action that thing performed. For instance, an eye would also mean "to see"; a hand, "to manage" or "to deal with"; a work tool, the trade with which it was associated. By simplifying and joining together groups of ideograms, the ancient Egyptians eventually formed two kinds of cursive writing: a hieratic, or "stately" form, used only for sacred texts, which required

Seated on a scaffold, a scribe decorates the architrave of a temple with pictographs that narrate histories of the dynasties and feats of pharaohs.

education and skill to understand, and a demotic, or common form, which was understood by everyone and used for diaries, work rosters, lists of products, and official decrees.

The Egyptians used a writing material made from the papyrus plant. Strips of the plant were pressed into sheets, which were then glued together and rolled on wooden rods to form scrolls.

Writing was held in high esteem in ancient Egypt, and to be a scribe meant belonging to a highly regarded profession. Many examples have been found of meticulously written scrolls that were kept in temples and royal palaces. Above all, scribes wrote about power and history, and Egyptian temples were full of hieroglyphics glorifying the feats of the pharaohs. This is why Egyptian priests thought the clever Greeks were like "lost children," for without writing they could not record their own origins and traditions. Writing is the memory of a people.

IDEOGRAMS AND THE WRITTEN ALPHABET

Humans create an amazing variety of signs and symbols. Animals, too, make signs, but they are "natural," such as tracks, odors, and secretions. Humans create signs and symbols using their intellect; these signs and symbols are designed to communicate, and the written word is the outstanding example. Humans have always left signs of their existence, from cave paintings to the decorations on the temples of the pharaohs to today's books, which use our alphabet. The history of written communication is marked off by different forms of expression using different systems of writing, from pictographs and cuneiform writing to hieroglyphics and runes and finally to our alphabet. The differences among these writing systems are enormous, but they can be divided into two main kinds: those using symbols and those using signs.

Pictographs, ideograms, and hierogly-

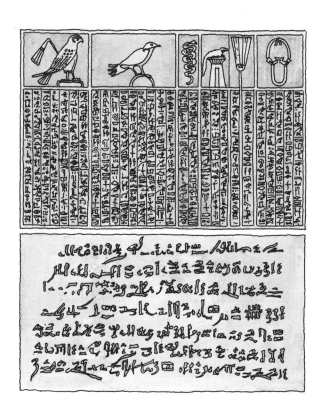

The Egyptians used three types of hieroglyphics: pictographs or ideograms, hieratic, and demotic. Pictographs were symbolic pictures, while hieratic and demotic were types of cursive writing.

Cuneiform writing was invented by the Sumerians and also used by the Babylonians. It used wedge-shaped strokes to form characters that were impressed in clay tablets.

phics cannot be precisely translated into spoken words. Each symbol or picture indicates a concept, a function, a profession, or an action. The Greeks made the decisive step to the use of a written alphabet around the seventh century B.C. Their alphabet, which became our own, was derived from that of the Phoenicians, who had reduced the number of signs to twenty-two. A system using pictographs or hieroglyphics is potentially infinite; a new symbol or picture can always be added. An alphabet is very different: the number of signs, meaning the number of letters, does not change; new words are added by making a new arrangement of letters. The other fundamental difference is that each letter of the alphabet has its own different vocal sound and written shape or form. Each consonant and each vowel has a written form that does not change.

The movement from using picture symbols to an alphabet was an important step in the simplification of communication. With the

Roman writing scratched on a wall. The similarity to our own writing is evident.

introduction of the alphabet, symbols lost their sacred character and became signs, straightforward written translations of spoken words. From this time on, writing was no longer secret or mysterious, as it had been in ancient Egypt. The signs written on paper or parchment could be read and understood by everyone.

Sacred texts and laws of the land were carved in stone and placed where they could be seen by everyone.

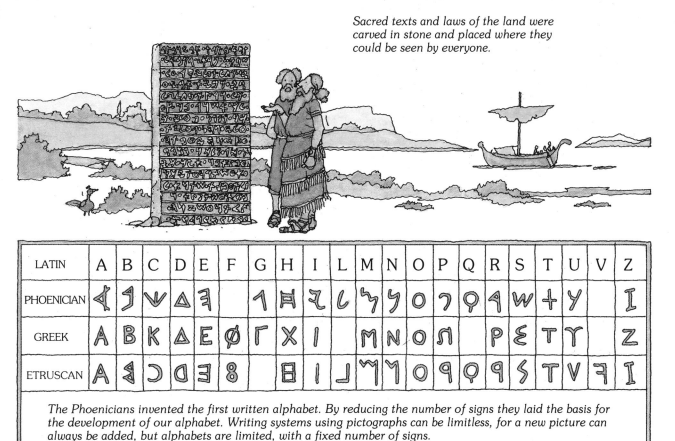

LATIN	A	B	C	D	E	F	G	H	I	L	M	N	O	P	Q	R	S	T	U	V	Z
PHOENICIAN																					
GREEK																					
ETRUSCAN																					

The Phoenicians invented the first written alphabet. By reducing the number of signs they laid the basis for the development of our alphabet. Writing systems using pictographs can be limitless, for a new picture can always be added, but alphabets are limited, with a fixed number of signs.

THE GREEK THEATER

Once a year there was a festival in Athens. It was a theatrical competition in which all the best authors presented their new plays. The theater was so important to the social life of ancient Greece that a government minister was assigned to organize the competitions with the help of several wealthy citizens.

There were two forms of Greek theater, comedy and tragedy. Tragedy had its origins in ancient rites celebrated to honor the gods. These rites involved a chorus that sang hymns and a lead singer, or actor, who participated in exchanges with the chorus. This tradition was further evolved by Aeschylus, who added a second actor, thus increasing the dramatic possibilities of tragedy. Sophocles continued this trend by adding a third actor and increasing the size

bitterness, and disillusions of everyday life.

The ancient religious rites that gave birth to tragedy also included boisterous choruses and dialogues, and these gave rise to comedy, which was further developed by popular farces. The greatest Greek writer of comedies was Aristophanes, whose works were examples of political, social, and literary satire. These works dealt with contemporary problems, such as war and peace, famine and abundance, and often made fun of the leading citizens of Athens.

Greek performances took place in open-air theaters. The stage was a circular area at the foot of a hill, and the audience sat on steps looking down. The actors wore masks that had metallic mouthpieces that increased the sound of their voices so that everyone could hear them.

When the performances ended, the

of the chorus. He also introduced painted scenery. In this way tragedy moved away from its religious origins and became representative of the relationships and stories that occur among ordinary, common people. Euripides, the third of the three great Greek writers of tragedy, took what his predecessors had developed and extended it even further. His tragedies depict the doubts,

The art called epigraphy involves writing on a hard material, such as marble or stone. The Romans made much use of this truly monumental form of communication.

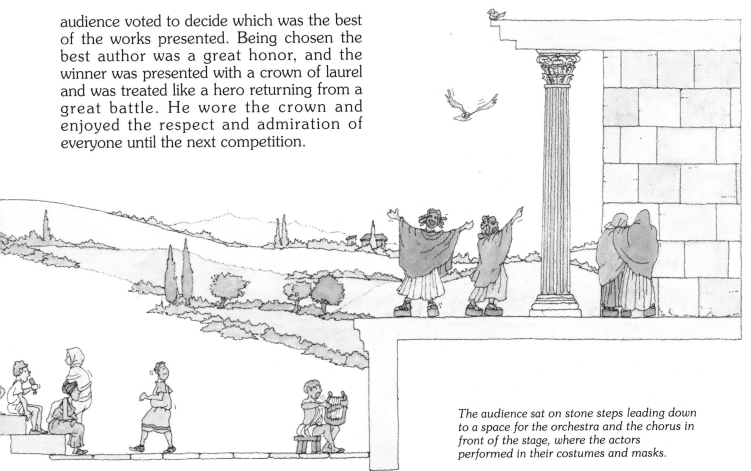

audience voted to decide which was the best of the works presented. Being chosen the best author was a great honor, and the winner was presented with a crown of laurel and was treated like a hero returning from a great battle. He wore the crown and enjoyed the respect and admiration of everyone until the next competition.

The audience sat on stone steps leading down to a space for the orchestra and the chorus in front of the stage, where the actors performed in their costumes and masks.

9

GREEK AND ROMAN SYMBOLS AND INSIGNIA

Nearly all ancient civilizations can be identified by some symbol that embodies the mysteries of that civilization's origins and is tied to a legendary episode in which history and myth are interwoven. For example, according to a Roman legend the twin brothers Romulus and Remus were found as babies and raised by a she-wolf; when Romulus founded the city of Rome, the wolf became the city's symbol, and the image of the wolf feeding the two boys was reproduced in countless works of art.

Besides such symbols there are insignia, which can be man-made structures or simple emblems that define a person's rank within a social group. The first kind of insignia includes the Greek and Roman stelae, which were stone slabs with inscriptions and sometimes carved scenes that were used as burial monuments. In the same category are the ancient Greek herms—rectangular stone pillars with the head of the god Hermes on top—which were used as road markers, since the god Hermes was believed to protect wayfarers. The Greek herms led to the portrait

busts made by the Romans, important steps in the evolution of portrait making.

Being an empire-building society with many dominions and borders to protect, ancient Rome depended on its military, and the Roman armies made much use of insignia. For many years the standards carried by Roman soldiers were decorated with pictures of various animals, but these

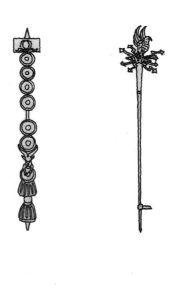

The Roman army made wide use of insignia. Each soldier carried a shield bearing the emblem of his unit, and each legion had its own emblem of which the soldiers were fiercely proud.

The head of Medusa, with snakes for hair, was a symbol of fear in ancient Greece.

Victory and progress are symbolized by the triskelion. The three-legged symbol was also used by the Celts.

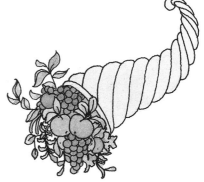

The cornucopia was a symbol of abundance and prosperity dear to the artists of the Italian Renaissance.

were eventually replaced by a single emblem, that of the eagle, symbol of strength and power. The eagle then became the enduring symbol of the Roman Empire. The different uniforms soldiers wore, as well as certain showy accessories, were insignia indicating their position and rank. Among the most famous insignia was the fasces, a bundle of rods around an axe, which was carried by the honor guards of magistrates as a symbol of their power and authority to punish any citizen or soldier found guilty of a crime.

Unlike a symbol, which stands for the unity of a civilization and often gives a sense of its atmosphere, an insignia emphasizes the differences among people, clearly stating the bearer's rank and power and designed to instill fear in enemies and give confidence to allies.

bust of Caius Marius

The ancient Romans had portraits made of themselves not just to preserve their own images for posterity, but also to show family likenesses and ties.

A Roman stonecutter in his workshop, working on a bust of a child of a nobleman's family.

bust of a woman

THE *ACTA DIURNA*

How was information exchanged in ancient Rome? For one thing, judges, scholars, and professors used codices, books composed of pages of parchment that were created by publishing houses. These and other books could also be found in public libraries.

Daily news of general interest, such as we get today from newspapers and television, was distributed by the magistrate who presided over the senate—the highest authority of the state. During the daily sitting of the senate, he took notes of the proceedings, which were then posted in public places. These *Acta Diurna* ("daily records") kept the public informed of all events in the senate, important political news, speeches made by important people and even simple gossip.

Students did their exercises with wax tablets, wooden boards covered with a layer of wax. They wrote in the wax with a pointed tool called a stylus; errors could be rubbed out, and the whole tablet could be scraped smooth and used again.

Public announcements of the senate's decisions and decrees kept the citizens informed of the actions taken by the senate each day and of decisions that would affect their lives.

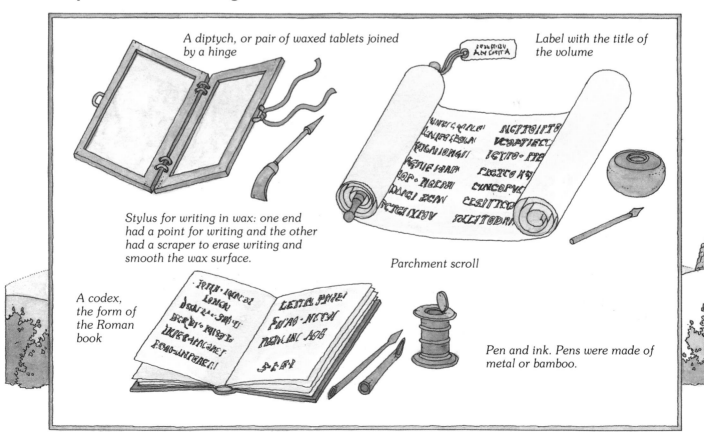

A diptych, or pair of waxed tablets joined by a hinge

Label with the title of the volume

Stylus for writing in wax: one end had a point for writing and the other had a scraper to erase writing and smooth the wax surface.

Parchment scroll

A codex, the form of the Roman book

Pen and ink. Pens were made of metal or bamboo.

THE ROMAN POSTAL SERVICE

Sending messages and dispatches was essential to keeping the provinces under control and ruling the empire. The *tabellarius*, or letter carrier, was the last link in the chain of the postal service of the Roman Empire. Driving a small two-wheeled horse-drawn cart, he traveled the roads from Bordeaux to Jerusalem, Cadiz to Brindisi, Wales to Greece, transporting orders and messages. The system was organized through rigid official channels. At the top was the prefect of the Praetorian Guard, assisted by inspectors, who supervised the application of the various rules. Then came a host of station masters at the many outlying way stations. These station masters checked the travel documents and permits of letter carriers and supervised the work of the blacksmiths and slaves who tended the stables where fresh horses were kept for the letter carriers.

Sending and receiving messages over long distances was of fundamental importance to the Romans. One method they used, especially the military, involved luminous signals produced by flaming torches. The torches would be arranged in two ordered rows in differing combinations that corresponded to different letters and numbers. This made it possible for someone at a distance, perhaps on a hilltop, to see and decode the message.

Torches lighted in the valleys pointed out the road.

The tabellarius *was the postman of ancient Rome. He traveled the roads of the empire carrying dispatches.*

At way stations the tabellarius *could stop, eat and drink, and change horses.*

RELIGIOUS SYMBOLS

Water, fire, a tree, a plow, a hatchet, a boat, a cross—we know these things because they are simple everyday items. But in the eyes of ancient people, these items had a strong symbolic meaning.

Symbols have a big advantage over words: they can express more, since they have much richer meanings. That is why Christianity, like all great religions, is based on them. The Old and New Testaments are expressed in symbolism and are thus always open to new interpretation. The plow is the symbol of creation; it breaks the soil so that people, symbolized as seeds, can grow. Heaven is portrayed as a wonderful garden, and the Church itself is often seen as a garden or park containing many different kinds of trees, which are the faithful followers of God. Planted in the garden is the Word, which is the Tree of Life, and Christ is the Word and the Tree of Life at one and the same time. Tied to the symbols of the garden and the tree is another image often used in Christian theology, that of the vineyard, where God is the winegrower who plants, tends, and gathers the fruit, and Christ is the trunk of the vine.

Another powerful symbol is water. The baptismal water represents God as the source of life and infers the presence of the Holy Spirit. Seen symbolically, water is that which gives life as opposed to that which brings death. This is why Christ is often represented symbolically as a fish,

People's strong religious sentiments during the Middle Ages were demonstrated by processions and the display of symbols that expressed their faith in the Church as God's representative on earth.

for he is revived and purified by contact with holy water. The cross is sometimes used as a symbol of Christianity, just as the star of David, or Magen David, can be a symbol of Judaism.

Symbols tell stories, open up new worlds of meaning. Sometimes the meaning of a symbol is based on old legends. Bees, for example, have always been a symbol of activity, diligence, and work. Because of the honey they make, bees are also a symbol of sweetness and eloquence. But people once believed that bees never sleep, so they were once also a symbol of vigilance and virtue.

TABLES OF THE LAW: The Ten Commandments written in stone

VIRGIN MARY (a heart pierced by a dagger): A symbol of the Virgin Mary, the grieving mother of Christ

AGNUS DEI (Lamb of God): The lamb represents an innocent victim and thus Christ, who died to save humankind.

INRI (Jesus Nazarenus Rex Judaeorum—Jesus of Nazareth, King of the Jews): Jesus was mocked and killed.

THE DOVE: The symbol of Easter, of life and resurrection

The pictures that adorn churches were usually painted outside and then later put in place inside.

SACRED STORIES AND THE ART OF PAINTING

A medieval person would look upward and see the fixed stars and the nine skies that were believed to separate people from the empyrean realm, the heavens, where angels and archangels, cherubim and seraphim were in charge of the movements of the skies. All these were proof of the power of God and the limitless perfection of his creations. Prayer and penitence and praising God gave sense and value to the lives of medieval people. Nobles retreated to monasteries to escape the temptations of earthly life. The long lines of flagellants, mendicant friars, and pilgrims traveling the countryside were seen as proof of the presence of God and the need for worship and prayer. Anyone who denied or even sought to question the greatness of God was considered a heretic and seen as an enemy. The guide for all people was the Catholic Church, whose mission was to inform everyone of the truth of the Gospel.

In every Christian country, churches, cathedrals, and sanctuaries were built to the greater glory and power of God. To the mere humans who looked up at them from the ground, these monstrous Romanesque and Gothic edifices must have seemed like huge arms outstretched to the sky.

The greatest painters of the time put their art into service for the glorification of God. Among the most famous early painters in Italy were Duccio di Buoninsegna, Simone

Martini, Cimabue, and above all Giotto, whom Dante mentioned in his *Divine Comedy,* praising his skill and fame. Art was thus a way of communicating sacred stories while at the same time celebrating them with beautiful illustrations of episodes from the Old and New Testaments or frescoes recounting the lives of saints.

Since most people of the Middle Ages could not read, these works of art were also intended to be educational, and since they were placed in churches and other public places, they could be seen and studied by everyone. Art taught people their own history so that they might be better able to follow the good example of their ancestors.

Many of these paintings can still be seen today, and just one look at a fresco by Giotto, a glance at the sweet and intense look on the face of the Madonna at the birth of Christ, is enough to make us understand in an instant the atmosphere of passion and mystery, of divinity and humanity, that was the Middle Ages.

COATS OF ARMS, FLAGS, TRUMPETS, DRUMS, AND BELLS

There were signals of war and peace. The bell called the faithful to mass or to war; it warned of danger when it rang the alarm. The trumpet was the instrument of the angels, announcing the glory of God, and heralds sounded their horns before reading the emperor's message.

The flag is a symbol, a colored display. The acrobatics of flag bearers, maintained unchanged for centuries, are still fascinating.

Even great artists like Dürer were inspired by heraldic themes. He designed this coat of arms for the Berghes family.

Every coat of arms bore a different emblem that stood for the family or house. Heraldry is the study of the meanings and history behind these emblems.

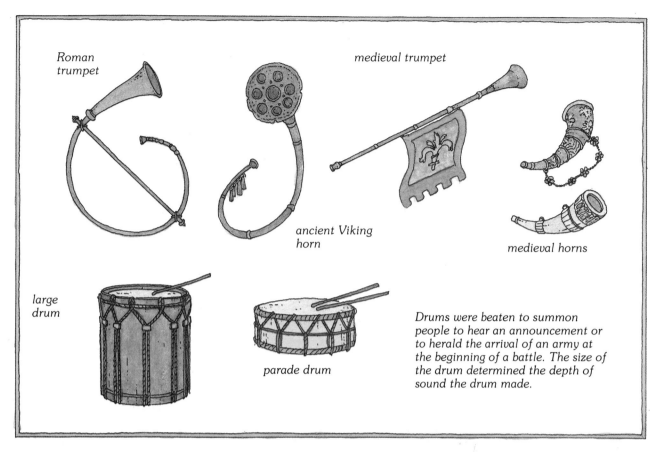

Roman trumpet

medieval trumpet

ancient Viking horn

medieval horns

large drum

parade drum

Drums were beaten to summon people to hear an announcement or to herald the arrival of an army at the beginning of a battle. The size of the drum determined the depth of sound the drum made.

Soldiers advanced into battle to the sound of beating drums. The cavalry charged carrying the flag of their ruler. The flag was sacred, having been blessed in a special church rite, so losing it in battle was considered a grave offense. The flag identified the army or community or even the feudal lord of the men who bore it. It signified war when unfurled during battle, but peace and fair play when unfurled during a tournament.

Cities were decorated with coats of arms on the doors, walls, and homes of the more illustrious families. Each coat of arms defined the lineage and importance of the family that it symbolized. Every word, every design, told the story of the family's origins and power; nothing on the coat of arms was there by chance. Each knight had his own coat of arms, composed of his family's coat of arms and special symbols, called devices, indicating his position in the family. Heralds, who had to recognize armored knights by the symbols on their shields, were trained to understand these devices.

The ringing of the bell announced the time of day.

CODICES AND MINIATURES

Ora et labora ("pray and work") was the rule of the ancient monastic orders, such as the Benedictines and Franciscans. The monks were kept busy all day in a constant stream of activities. Through prayer and work they served and honored God. In the peace and quiet of monastery libraries, monks copied and transcribed ancient texts. Thanks to the tireless labors of these monks many texts from ancient Greece and Rome survived the barbarian invasions and the hard times of the Middle Ages and are still available to us today.

It was the job of the amanuensis (copyist) to do this very difficult and important job. The manuscripts were usually very large and similar to the books we see on lecterns in public libraries. The copyists wrote on parchment made of sheepskin or goatskin that had been worked until it was as thin as

Inside a monastery. At every table a monk was busy with a particular job.

20

paper. Different skills were needed. Some monks specialized in preparing the parchment, and some did the calligraphy, or handwriting. Then there were the miniaturist and the binder. The miniaturist created paintings and decorations on the first page of the book and also at the beginning of each paragraph and alongside the columns of writing. This painting was done using powdered gold and silver dissolved in water and mixed with gum arabic. (The word *miniaturist* derives from the Latin *minium,* a powdered red lead that artists used extensively in their designs for its bright red color.)

The last operation was that of the binder. Each codex, or manuscript book, was composed of many separate sheets of parchment folded in the center and then sewn together. Both the folding, performed using a flat wooden bar, and the sewing were done by hand. Later, as the demand for books increased, the books were sewn by machine.

No other object gives as clear a sense of the Middle Ages and the atmosphere of medieval monasteries as a manuscript book. The beautiful miniatures evoke the quiet labor, the humility, but also the great artistic skill of the nameless monks who considered their work a form of continuous prayer. The parchment pages, often thick and coarse, bear witness to the difficult and damp conditions in which the monks often had to work. Their unfailing patience and dedication are evident in the beautiful handwriting using Gothic characters that they produced.

The ever-increasing number of Christian churches springing up all over Europe made a great demand for copies of the Scriptures, books by Church fathers, and liturgical texts necessary for daily church services. Besides such theological texts, there were encyclopedias and books used for the training of professional clergymen. The very structure of these books reflects the way in which they were used. Later on, smaller, more easily transportable books were made for the use of university students and city businessmen; but the books made during the early Middle Ages served other purposes. To monks and other people, the text of a book was

absolutely inseparable from the commentaries added to the book by those who used it. In fact, the pages of early codices had ample room for the addition of commentaries—the text was located in two columns down the center of the page, leaving the outer areas blank. People read books slowly, studying the commentaries and meditating on the meaning. In truth, writing, decorating, and studying books were only different ways of praying and acknowledging the greatness of God.

In ancient medieval codices the writing is never detached from the designs and the decoration.

From the Middle Ages until the invention of printing, the illuminated and illustrated book was a work of art.

During the Renaissance, illustrations lost their instructional nature, were less related to the text—and became works of art.

Antiphonaries were books containing the choral parts of liturgical services.

MINSTRELS, STROLLING PLAYERS, AND BALLADEERS

There was bustle and noise in the town square, where many people were listening to music and admiring the colored costumes of dancers. This was a festival of minstrels and strolling players, of balladeers and troubadours. Although medieval roads were fraught with danger and little used, this new social group wandered tirelessly among cities and villages. They were wandering university students, traveling clergymen, and poor students who simply followed some master. Some were minstrels who played at court; others were musicians and singers; and a few were the ever-popular jesters. Their stage was any village square or threshing floor. Living by their wits and by begging, they carried the message of a new culture, different from the everyday one. Using rhythm and music, storytelling and their great skills at mime, they found their own way to broadcast their message.

In medieval times there was no radio, television, or cinema, and in small settlements not even a theater. To break the monotony of daily life, people were happy to gather in town squares to listen to the amazing stories and adventures told by balladeers.

WOODCUTS, ENGRAVINGS, AND INCUNABULA

Printing—stamping marks onto a surface—is an important means of communication. Woodcuts, in which a design is cut into wood to make a kind of stamp, are the oldest method of printmaking and were first used for stamping patterns on textiles. Woodcuts are done by cutting a design into wood with a gouge and chisel. All the wood that will not be part of the final image is cut away to leave the design raised above the surface. By inking the woodcut and then pressing a sheet of paper against it a print could be made. Other

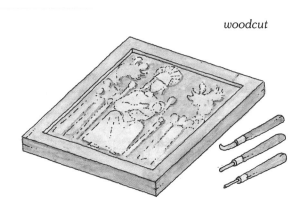

woodcut

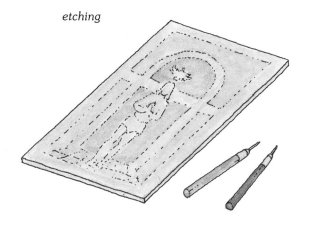

burins

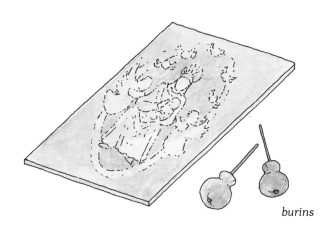

etching

methods of printmaking include engraving and etching. In engraving, the design is inscribed on a sheet of copper, zinc, or brass with an engraving tool called a burin. Etching is done by covering a copper sheet with wax and drawing the image into the wax with a sharp tool. The sheet is dipped in nitric acid, which burns the scratched line into the copper. The longer the acid is left to work, the deeper the lines, making it possible to achieve shading. Another method is lithography, in which the image is drawn on a flat stone with a wax crayon or grease ink. When the stone is inked, the ink adheres to the drawn image, which can then be printed on paper.

An art dealer and printer examining the quality of the finished work from a hand-operated printing press in one of the many workshops that were set up throughout Europe toward the middle of the fifteenth century.

The revolution in printing came with the invention of movable type. As with many great inventions, several people claimed the invention as their own, but history names the inventor of movable type as Johann Gutenberg, a craftsman who worked in Mainz, Germany, in the middle of the fifteenth century. Gutenberg's idea was to make many copies of each letter of the alphabet out of metal so that the letters could be put together to form words and columns of text. The letters could be used over and over again, making it possible to make many copies of books. The invention of movable type was a decisive turning point in communications. A monk had to labor many days to create a single copy of a manuscript, but with movable type the pages of a book could be quickly assembled, and each page could be reproduced an infinite number of times. The earliest printed books are called incunabula, from a Latin word meaning "cradle," for they were made during the infancy of printing.

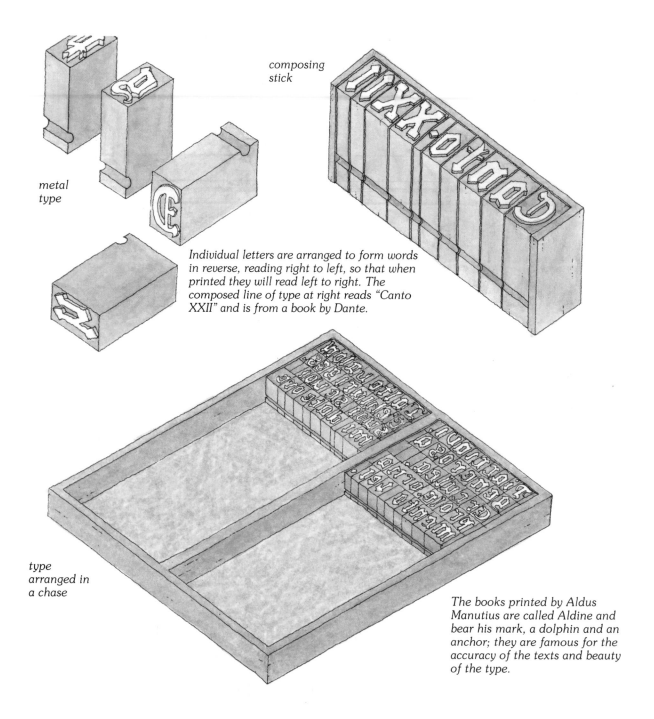

metal type

composing stick

Individual letters are arranged to form words in reverse, reading right to left, so that when printed they will read left to right. The composed line of type at right reads "Canto XXII" and is from a book by Dante.

type arranged in a chase

The books printed by Aldus Manutius are called Aldine and bear his mark, a dolphin and an anchor; they are famous for the accuracy of the texts and beauty of the type.

MOVABLE TYPE

In a very short time, Gutenberg's invention became widespread, and new printing shops began to spring up. The first ones were set up in Germany, but after about 1465 this new art was introduced all over Europe, and various cities became famous for their printers. In 1498 Aldus Manutius published a five-volume set of the Greek classics in Venice and gained immediate fame as a printer. He was especially interested in making small books for scholars at low cost, and to save space in his books he designed a style of type based on handwriting that today is known as *italics*, because it came from Italy.

Each great discovery heralds a new era. With the invention of printing, books lost their character as precious and rare works of art created by monks and copyists and became instead objects readily available to an increasing number of people. Far from the monastic libraries, books began to circulate. They became familiar objects that could be bought or exchanged and loved by everyone.

PRINTING FROM MOVABLE TYPE

The Bible was the first book printed in Gutenberg's workshop and thus the first printed book. Gutenberg used a wooden press, a crucible over a small fire to melt the metal from which he cast his type letters, and a tilted wooden case with many small compartments to hold his type. A different letter of the alphabet was in each compartment. The printer composed the line of type word by word on a composing stick, separating the individual words with pieces of metal and spacing the words to fill the line length. When he had enough lines to make a page, he placed them in a metal frame called a chase and locked them into place using metal wedges called quoins. The chase was then clamped in place on the press and ink was spread over the type using leather daubers or a roller (printer's ink is thick and sticky, not thin like the writing ink used in pens). The chase was then covered with a sheet of paper and slid under the horizontal platen of the press. By turning a lever, pressure was applied, pushing the inked type against the paper. The printed sheet would then be lifted off the press and hung up to let the ink dry.

Gutenberg examined the first page of print of his Bible with a critical eye. Behind the master sat a member of the new profession of typographer.

Type case: the divided tray for holding individual letters

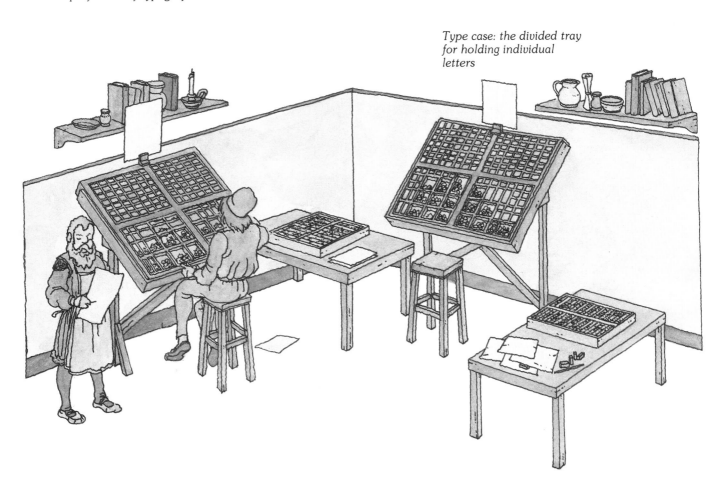

Printing a page with a hand press

1) The chase with its type is placed face-up on the carriage of the press, and the type is inked. The sheet of paper to be printed is placed in a frame.

3) By turning the lever on the screw, pressure is applied to the platen, which pushes the paper against the inked type in the chase.

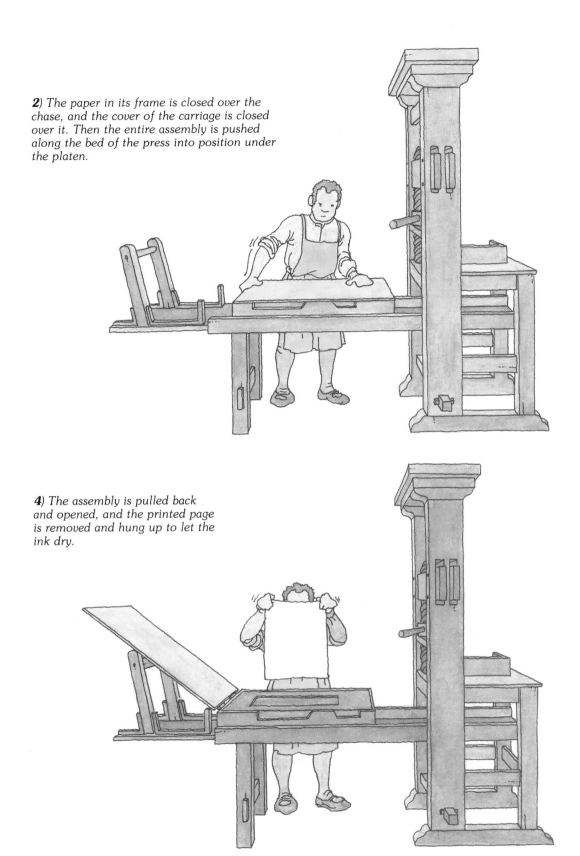

2) *The paper in its frame is closed over the chase, and the cover of the carriage is closed over it. Then the entire assembly is pushed along the bed of the press into position under the platen.*

4) *The assembly is pulled back and opened, and the printed page is removed and hung up to let the ink dry.*

NEWSPAPERS AND JOURNALS

As printing shops sprang up everywhere, a new phenomenon of great importance began to appear: the first printed newspapers and journals. In addition to the daily news and cultural topics, these carried informative and educational items. The number of readers was steadily growing, and people were eager to read newspapers, magazines, reviews, and criticism. Today we are bombarded by information and facts from around the world—reading allows us to look beyond the place we live and discover new horizons.

The precursors of the modern newspaper were private letters that passed among international merchants, but little of the information in these would have been of interest to the general public. The first gazettes reported business news of no great importance, notices from foreign courts, and what we call today "yellow journalism," stories of fires and storms, miraculous cures,

The habit of reading newspapers took hold all over Europe, and people discussed the great news stories and the items of everyday interest with friends and neighbors.

Local journals appeared in almost all cities. The Gazzetta di Parma in Italy was unusual in that it changed from being a weekly to being a daily newspaper.

Together with the typographer, the profession of editor was born—a difficult and complex job that had never been seen before.

and murders. The ability of newspapers to spread information was immediately clear to rulers, who often took over gazettes and turned them into government newspapers.

The first magazines appeared toward the end of the seventeenth century. Instead of news, these carried commentaries and were designed to be educational. Some magazines dealt with moral issues that were discussed publicly in cafes and bars; readers sent letters to the editor, some of which were printed. Other magazines printed articles of scientific interest; others contained book reviews and essays on cultural events. There were also almanacs, handy and dependable collections of information, including notations of anniversaries and interesting facts, home medical advice, statistics of all sorts, and jokes. The variety of printed matter grew as the reading public grew, and increasing numbers of people were drawn to magazines as sources of entertainment and education.

From medieval manuscripts to printed books and finally to newspapers, the new overtook the old. Some professions disappeared and new ones appeared; typographers took the place of monks in the creation of books. The printing of books, newspapers, and magazines of all sorts became a large-scale industry with a new organization designed to create printed matter and distribute it to an enormous public.

THE TYPEWRITER

The idea of replacing handwriting with machine writing long fascinated many people. The changing demands of business and the general taste for machines and

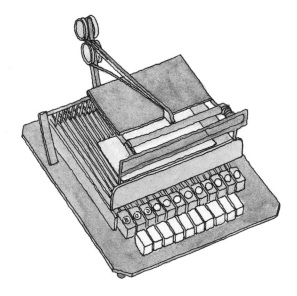

Certain aspects of the writing cembalo of 1837 were later employed in the modern typewriter.

automation eventually led to the invention of the typewriter. The first machine with a keyboard and levers was the so-called tachygrapher, invented about 1823. Another precursor of the typewriter was the writing cembalo, invented by an Italian named Giuseppe Ravizza in 1837. It had suspended levers that struck upward and, most important, a moving carriage.

In 1874 the Remington company presented the first practical typewriter and immediately put it into mass production. The new machine caught on fast: just one year later Mark Twain used a Remington typewriter to write *The Adventures of Tom Sawyer*, making him the first author to use a typewriter.

The first heavy manual typewriters soon gave way to portable machines and electric typewriters, and today writing is also done on computers. The fast, precise click-clack of the keyboard is very much a part of our modern world—it has submerged forever the silence of the ancient copyists.

A modern manual typewriter

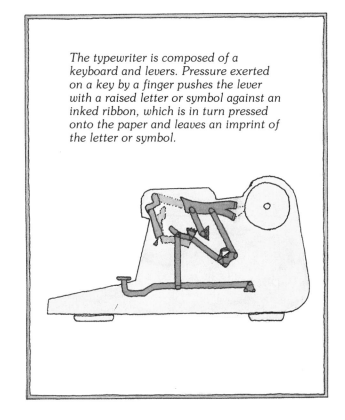

The typewriter is composed of a keyboard and levers. Pressure exerted on a key by a finger pushes the lever with a raised letter or symbol against an inked ribbon, which is in turn pressed onto the paper and leaves an imprint of the letter or symbol.

THE PHOTOGRAPH

A racing car speeding by, a running dog, someone blowing out the candles on a birthday cake: with just a click, a simple movement of a finger on the shutter release of a camera, a moment in time is fixed forever. A photograph gives us the ability to stop time, to bear faithful witness to a situation, to remember past feelings when we see our own face, our captured emotions. Every time we look at a photograph, we are able to relive the moment, to bring the past into the present.

Between 1830 and 1850, this new invention was seen as something truly extraordinary; everywhere the cry could be heard, "From now on, painting is dead." Pictures made with a camera depicted the exact truth without the intervention of the artist's hand. At this time the camera was an enormous wooden box mounted on a tripod, and it produced a picture called a daguerreotype, named after its inventor, Louis Jacques Mandé Daguerre. The photographs were taken using a tin plate prepared with silver chloride, which needed a very long exposure time. The subject had to sit very still in front of the camera for three or four minutes before the image was created on the tin plate.

The development of photographic technology led quickly to improvements in the camera and the materials used. In 1840, the first camera lens was introduced, enabling the photographer to focus the image. The tin plate went out of use with the introduction of paper that was treated with a gelatin and silver halides. This paper produced much clearer prints with a much

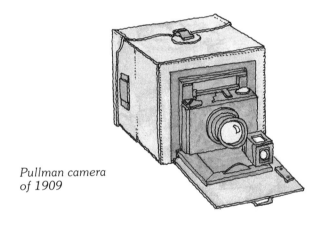

Pullman camera of 1909

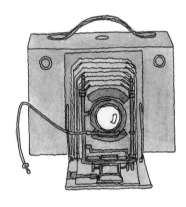

Kodak camera of 1910

In a typical photographic studio in America at the end of the nineteenth century: the subject is being photographed wearing an Indian headdress against a painted backdrop of the Rocky Mountains.

33

shorter exposure time, but the real revolution happened at the end of the 1800s, when this paper was replaced by celluloid film.

The introduction of the halftone process in 1881 made it possible for photographs to be reproduced accurately in newspapers and books. Then in 1888 George Eastman introduced roll film and the simple Kodak box camera, making photography available to everyone and leading to the birth of modern photography.

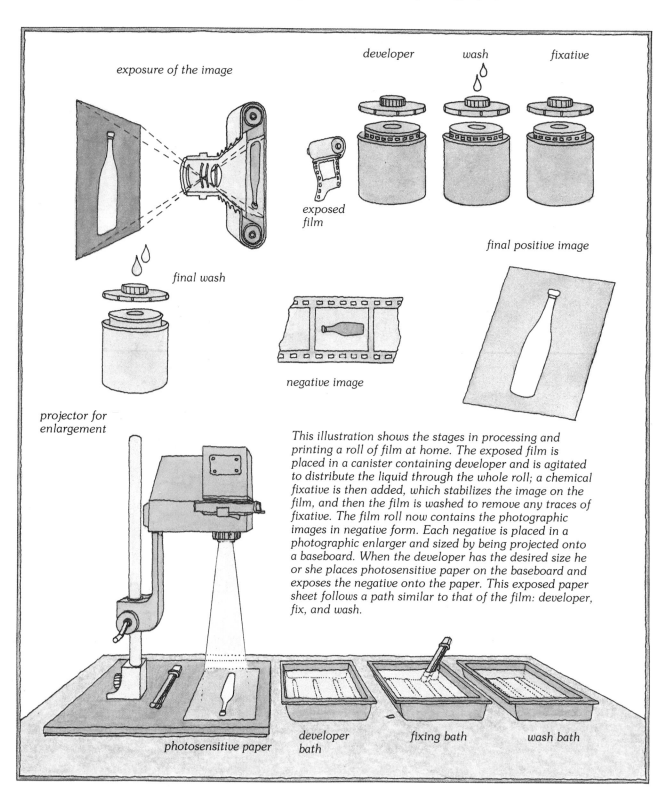

exposure of the image

developer   wash   fixative

exposed film

final wash

final positive image

negative image

projector for enlargement

This illustration shows the stages in processing and printing a roll of film at home. The exposed film is placed in a canister containing developer and is agitated to distribute the liquid through the whole roll; a chemical fixative is then added, which stabilizes the image on the film, and then the film is washed to remove any traces of fixative. The film roll now contains the photographic images in negative form. Each negative is placed in a photographic enlarger and sized by being projected onto a baseboard. When the developer has the desired size he or she places photosensitive paper on the baseboard and exposes the negative onto the paper. This exposed paper sheet follows a path similar to that of the film: developer, fix, and wash.

photosensitive paper   developer bath   fixing bath   wash bath

THE MODERN POSTAL SYSTEM

You see them on the top right-hand corner of envelopes, with their beautiful colors and designs. They carry portraits of presidents, show famous monuments, record important events. They are postage stamps, first introduced in England in 1840 by Rowland Hill, a post office official who invented adhesive stamps when he was reforming the English postal system. In a very short time postage stamps went into use throughout the world.

The use of stamps was an important landmark in the history of postal systems. Today the world has become a very small place, and the need for communication and the exchange of information and merchandise has become urgent. The world's postal services have changed to meet those needs. Public and private agencies deliver mail by land, sea, and most of all air. People everywhere want speed and reliability.

Since their introduction in 1840, postage stamps have been items of interest and study. The collection and study of postage stamps is called philately. The first printed stamp catalog was issued in France in 1861.

Packages or letters can reach even the most faraway places in just a few hours.

The rapid technological evolution of the telephone kept pace with aesthetic developments, as can be seen from the Meucci prototype (left) and the Ericson model (right).

THE TELEPHONE

In every shape, size, and color, fixed or portable, at home, in the office, or in the car, the phone is never very far away. Our voice can reach anyone, anywhere and anytime we want. The entire world has become a huge network of communication.

The invention of the telephone caused a great deal of controversy and a long court battle between Antonio Meucci, an Italian living on Long Island, and Alexander Graham Bell as to who should be granted the patent for the invention. In the end, Meucci's priority was recognized, while Bell received the world's recognition and remuneration. These men and others were the pioneers of

this aspect of the modern world, and they all greatly contributed to the expansion of our horizons.

The telephone, like the telegraph, was designed to take advantage of electricity. Anything that moves emits a noise, which is caused by vibrations in the air around it. This also happens when we speak. The task of the telephone is to transmit the vibrations of speech into an electric current and send that current along a wire to a receiver, which then transforms it back into recognizable sounds. Since an electric current can travel over a far greater distance than a voice can, we now have a means to talk to someone very far away. In just a few years after the telephone was patented communicating with this device

When you lifted the hand receiver and dialed a number, you put yourself in contact with . . .

a switchboard located in your area, where an operator quickly transferred the call to . . .

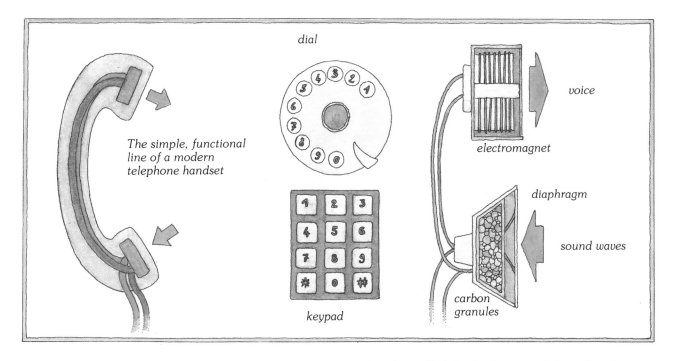

dial

The simple, functional line of a modern telephone handset

electromagnet

voice

diaphragm

sound waves

carbon granules

keypad

Above right: Sound waves from a voice generate vibrations in a thin plate called the diaphragm and through carbon granules. These vibrations induce an electric current, which travels to the receiver of the telephone being called, where it activates an electromagnet; the vibrations of the current through another diaphragm reproduce the caller's voice.

had increased dramatically, and the crackly old phones of Meucci and Bell had been improved beyond recognition. Soon the first switchboards to transfer calls had been introduced. It is impossible today to conceive of a world without phones. It would be like a bad science fiction story or dream: everyone would be isolated, condemned to speak only to the few people around them.

a switchboard in the receiver's area. The operator there sent the electrical impulse of your call . . .

to the receiver's telephone, which rang. Someone picked up the phone, and you were ready to begin your conversation.

THE TELEGRAPH

When the first telegraph line, which ran between Baltimore and Washington, was constructed, the newspapers of the day made headlines of this sensational new invention by Samuel Morse. It was the first practical application of research in the general use of electricity. The idea was to transmit information over long distances by a system whereby each letter of the alphabet was represented by a combination of only two different signs—dots and dashes. These signs corresponded to electric impulses. A short impulse stood for a dot; an impulse three times longer was a dash. Once this code, the Morse code, was established, telegraphists could send and receive messages and decode the dots and dashes into the languages we use.

The telegraph consists of a transmitting device that sends the message on its way in the form of electrical impulses of different lengths.

The receiving apparatus translates the signals into an ordered succession of dots and dashes.

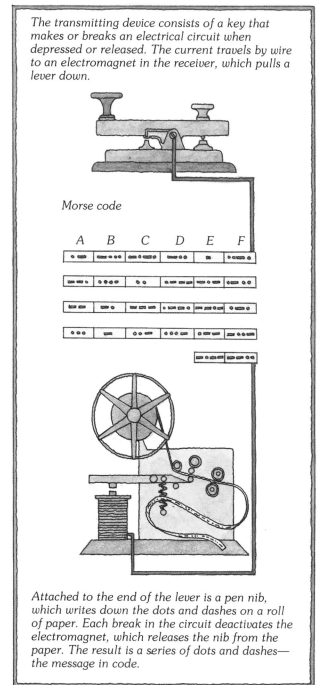

The transmitting device consists of a key that makes or breaks an electrical circuit when depressed or released. The current travels by wire to an electromagnet in the receiver, which pulls a lever down.

Morse code

A	B	C	D	E	F

Attached to the end of the lever is a pen nib, which writes down the dots and dashes on a roll of paper. Each break in the circuit deactivates the electromagnet, which releases the nib from the paper. The result is a series of dots and dashes— the message in code.

THE WIRELESS TELEGRAPH

On December 6, 1901, Guglielmo Marconi received a telegraph signal from Cornwall, England. The agreed signal was the letter S, three dots in Morse code. The astonishing thing was that Marconi was nearly two thousand miles away, in Canada. The message was sent without wires or relay stations, and from then on scientific research centered on ways to transmit messages through the air.

We owe a huge debt to Marconi for his scientific experiments, but without the existing research work of the Scottish physicist James Clerk Maxwell and the German Heinrich Hertz, Marconi's invention would have been impossible. Maxwell

theorized that a variable electric current generated electromagnetic waves that were of the same nature as light waves, but were invisible. That is to say, they traveled through space in the same way and at the same speed as light. Hertz demonstrated the existence of these electromagnetic waves by generating radio waves (which are electromagnetic) in a laboratory using an oscillating current. It has often happened in history that a scientist makes a discovery but is unable to imagine its practical application. So it was that Maxwell's theory and Hertz's experiments gave Marconi the idea of using these electromagnetic waves to transmit messages around the world.

The notion that radio waves could follow the curvature of the earth met with much skepticism and disbelief—some people thought the signals would be lost in the air. By successfully transmitting the signal S from one side of the world to the other,

The wireless telegraph was first used for civilian purposes, such as helping ships in distress.

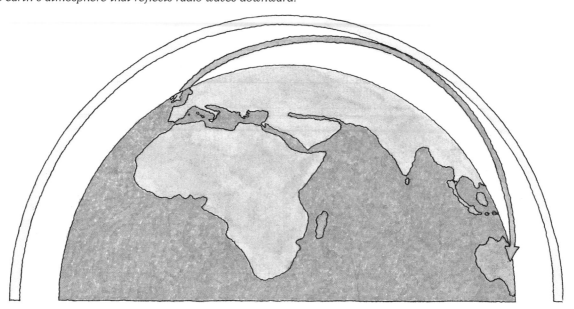

Marconi laid all such doubts to rest. A short time later, scientists provided an explanation for Marconi's success by demonstrating the existence of the ionosphere, a layer of ionized air which, by reflecting radio waves back to earth, makes long-distance wireless communication possible.

The wireless telegraph had many immediate and practical uses. Marconi himself actively promoted it as an aid for ships in distress, and so his invention was first used for humanitarian purposes. Clearly a new era was under way, one in which the vast, unknown world was destined to become as accessible as any small village.

The world gets smaller. People were astonished when Marconi transmitted an electrical signal from England to Adelaide, Australia, that turned on the city's lights.

THE PHONOGRAPH

"Mary had a little lamb, its fleece was white as snow." The words of the nursery rhyme were the first sounds played by a phonograph, and although the voice was crackly, it was recognizably that of the machine's inventor, Thomas Alva Edison. Edison's machine used cylinders, but ten years later the gramophone appeared, which used a metal disk covered with wax. Later still, through the use of electric amplifiers, the sound produced became clearer and louder, and plastic replaced the metal disks. Today, the vinyl album has been replaced by compact disks on which digital information is read by a laser beam.

The first phonographs gave a very distorted sound of limited volume. The introduction of the amplifier was a great improvement, compensating for the distortion and increasing the volume.

1903 (Columbia)

1893 (Berliner)

The wind-up phonograph was invented by Thomas Edison in 1877 and later perfected by Emile Berliner. It consisted of a speaker horn, a needle, and a handle that had to be cranked to wind up the spring-driven motor that turned the record.

THE MOVIE CAMERA

Imagine a little white screen at the front of the room with the flickering image of a train coming toward us and then a door opening and a line of factory workers filing out. On the evening of December 28, 1895, in Paris, the spectators who attended the Grand Café to see the Lumière brothers' first picture show were thrilled and sometimes jolted out of their seats by the movements on the little screen. On that evening, in that darkened room, the history of the cinema began. The new form of entertainment was destined, in a very short time, to change the lives, leisure time, and even the way of thinking of people throughout the world. Cinematic technology improved rapidly, and today the movie camera of the Lumière brothers would not be out of place in an archaeological museum.

It was immediately clear that movies are an extraordinary vehicle for ideas. They show movement, living people, and thus life itself. At first, the most popular films were comedies and stories from history about important people, wars, and epic struggles—stories from books that came to life on the silver screen. The arrival of sound movies at the end of the 1920s caused a revolution in cinema. Sound made possible new kinds of cinema: comedies, melodramas, musicals. The movie camera could tell stories about men and women with which people everywhere could identify. There was the bowler and cane of Charlie Chaplin as the Tramp, the sometimes sweet and sometimes proud cartoon characters of Walt Disney, the travels and adventures of science fiction heroes. The cinema is an art; the dreams it creates are so large that they become part of our lives.

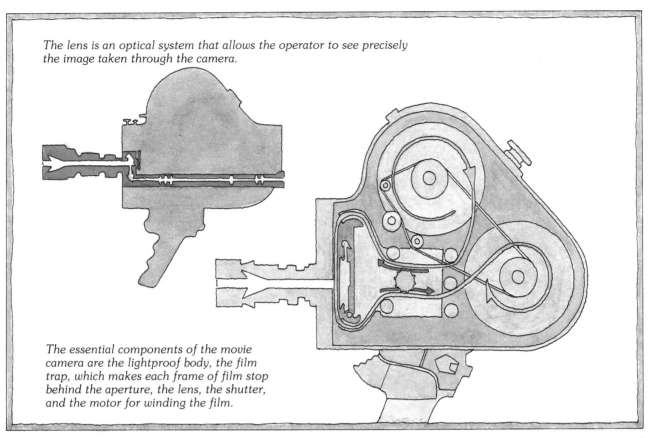

The lens is an optical system that allows the operator to see precisely the image taken through the camera.

The essential components of the movie camera are the lightproof body, the film trap, which makes each frame of film stop behind the aperture, the lens, the shutter, and the motor for winding the film.

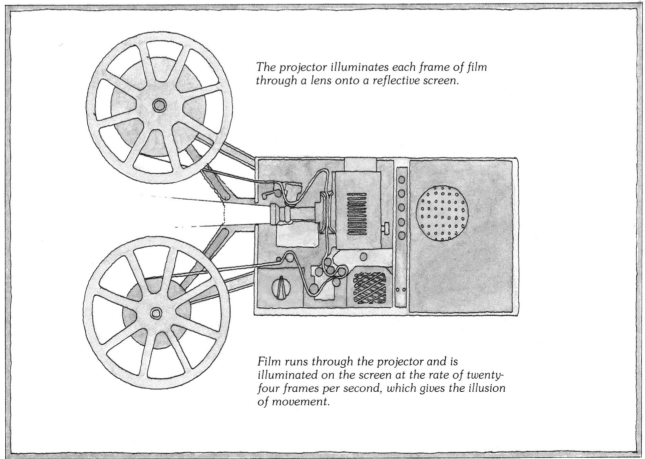

The projector illuminates each frame of film through a lens onto a reflective screen.

Film runs through the projector and is illuminated on the screen at the rate of twenty-four frames per second, which gives the illusion of movement.

MAKING A FILM

Let's go behind the scenes to meet all the people whom we never really see but who are involved in the making of a film. We know about actors and directors, but before their work can begin, authors and screenwriters have to do their part. They create the idea for the film, write the plot and introduce the characters, and then approach a producer with their ideas. He or she is the real star in the organization of the whole movie. The producer must choose and approve the movie's subject, find the money for producing it, choose the director, and preside over every aspect of the movie-making. The producer's staff may include production directors, production inspectors, and a production secretary.

The director is responsible for the artistic side of the film; he or she too will have assistants, the most important of whom is the assistant director, who is regarded as the director's right arm. The set designer, the cinematographer, or director of photography, the musical director, the sound technicians,

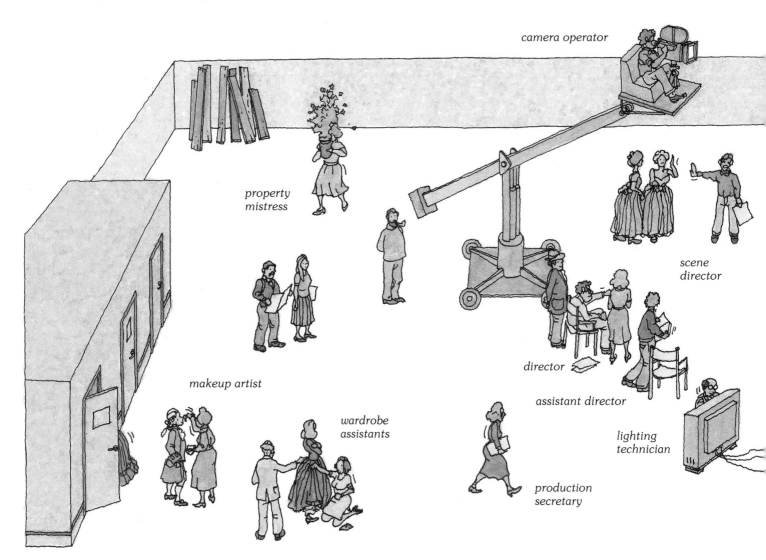

camera operator

property mistress

scene director

director

assistant director

makeup artist

wardrobe assistants

lighting technician

production secretary

Here we are on the film set. Everything is ready; the actors are in position and waiting. When the director calls, "Action!" the clapper boards sound and the first take begins.

and the editor all have their own teams of assistants. The set designer employs people to build the sets; the cinematographer, who is in charge of lighting the sets and photographing the film, is assisted by camera operators and electricians; the assistant director coordinates the work of the entire film crew. Also on call are the costume designers, makeup artists, hairdressers and a host of other assistants, such as gaffers (chief electricians) and grips (general workers), runners and technicians, accountants, publicity people, and a vast army of caterers, drivers, stunt people, and extras.

production assistant

actors

set builders

workman

THE RADIO

Just a click of a button, a twist of a dial, and the talking machine immediately starts working, filling the house with words, sounds, and music. Together with the telephone, the telegraph, and the television, the radio is an instrument that has helped to make the world a little smaller, making faraway places seem familiar and nearby. The telegraph was soon rendered out of date by the introduction of radio.

"One, two, three . . . on the air!" The speaker is the voice of the radio. It bids you good morning, keeps you company throughout the day, and at the end of the day wishes you good night. A voice from far away, it is always close by.

Experiments in the electronic transmission of speech and music began in 1904, and after several years of study and many new inventions, the first commercial broadcasting station in the United States, KDKA at Pittsburgh, was established. Many radio broadcast "firsts" quickly followed: the first concert (1920), the first news program (1920), the first baseball game (1921), the first weather broadcast (1921).

Radio was an immediate, enormous, and unstoppable success, and the radio receiver became a standard household fixture. News, messages, financial reports, and information of every kind were soon being broadcast all over the world. Advertisements started changing the lives of millions of people. Suddenly, people felt as though they were part of a larger community and not just a small village or town. Peace and war, the crucial events that changed history, but also sports events and symphonies and other moments of joy or entertainment no longer occurred in distant places that were hard to imagine but took place live, just as they happened, in the living room of every listener.

How was all of this made possible? The same discoveries concerning electro-

magnetic waves that helped Marconi discover the telegraph led to the invention of the radio. The radio works by using a microphone to transform the sound waves that are produced every time we speak into electromagnetic waves of variable strength, which are sent into space by a transmitter. These waves are picked up by a receiving antenna and converted into impulses identical to those in the transmitting microphone. The vibrations on the diaphragm of a speaker reproduce the sound waves, and out comes the sound, exactly as it was at the source.

Development of radio technology brought many changes. In particular the transistor, invented just after World War II, made radios smaller and more portable. Portable radios and car radios came into common use.

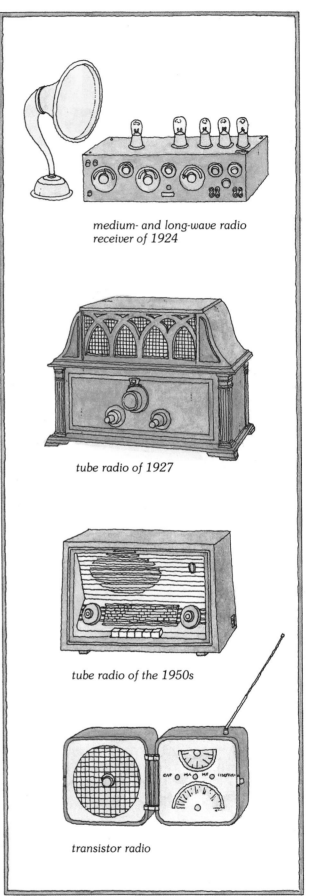

medium- and long-wave radio receiver of 1924

tube radio of 1927

tube radio of the 1950s

transistor radio

MAKING A NEWSPAPER

Weeklies, biweeklies, monthlies—every day many different kinds of publications arrive at newsstands. They put on a splendid show with all their glossy colorful covers. Newspapers, however, have a very different life. They are bought and read just a few hours included in the next day's edition are made in the early afternoon, and later all the stories written or sent in by reporters and correspondents come in. By 8:00 P.M. the newspaper is roughly blocked out to show where each story, headline, photograph, and advertisement will go in the final edition. News items continue to arrive, and

publisher

assistant editors

foreign news editor

copy editors

sports editor

local news editor

section heads

messenger

after the news happens. The news office always has an open door on the world. The publisher's job is to oversee the general running of the office; together with the editors, he or she selects the news to be included and makes sure that it gets written up and printed on time. Every daily paper has section heads, who are responsible for preparing the items included in their section: politics, local news, foreign news, sports, and entertainment. The hours in a news office pass in frenetic activity. Decisions about which news items are to be

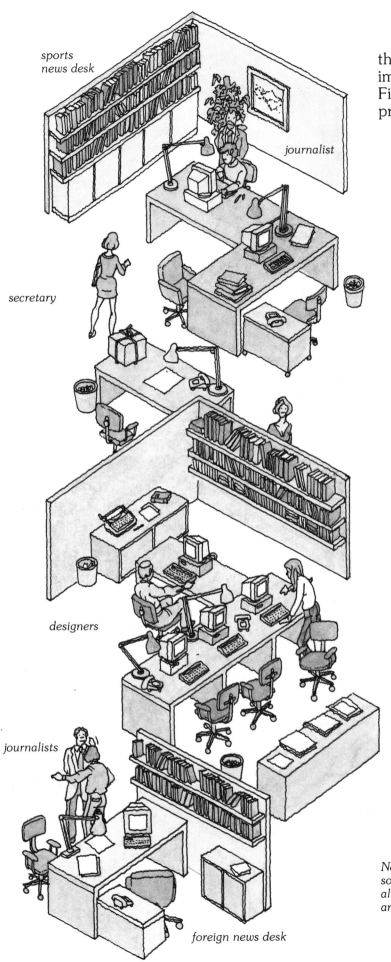

sports
news desk

journalist

secretary

designers

journalists

foreign news desk

the layout is changed to make room for important updates until the very last minute. Finally, the newspaper is put to bed— printed.

editors

page makeup

Newspaper offices are noisy and exciting: something is always happening, there is always some new story to discuss, explain, and write about.

PRINTING A NEWSPAPER

Once upon a time newspapers were made in print shops full of busy typesetters and journalists and the smell of ink and clatter of Linotype machines. The news arrived on calibrated paper or galley pages; the newspaper was set in type and then printed.

Technological progress and computerization have brought about a real revolution in printing processes and methods. Gone are typewriters, replaced by computers. Journalists write their articles on computers, use keyboard commands to specify the size of type, headlines, subheads, and the position of the stories on the page, and then send the articles electronically to a central terminal. The pages and sections of the newspaper are then laid out. Once this was done by typesetters using Linotype machines and metal type; today it is done using the images on computer screens, which are then used to

create photoengraved plates. The newspaper is printed on rotary presses, and in a short time copies are ready for distribution to delivery people and newsstands.

Technological progress is taking place so rapidly that the newspaper industry seems destined for further, unpredictable changes.

In the future, newspapers may not even be made of paper. Just as the dusty old newspaper archives have been replaced by tiny magnetic disks that store information, so newspapers may someday be replaced by computer disks bearing information updated just a few moments ago.

Uses of the main printing systems

flexography:
for printing on packages, wallpaper, wrapping paper

offset lithography:
for magazines and catalogs; usually for up to 200,000 copies

rotogravure:
for magazines and catalogs; usually for up to 300,000 copies

web offset lithography:
for illustrated books and high-quality printing

Flexographic printing

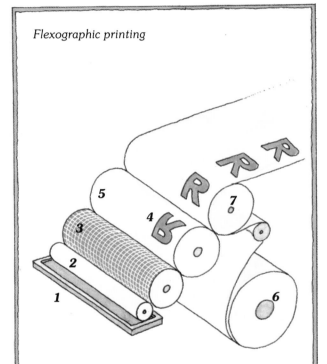

The ink held in a basin (1) is picked up on the rubber ink roller (2); the screen cylinder (3) presses against this, and any excess ink is removed by a wiper blade. After being inked, the line-cut block (4) on the print cylinder (5) prints the image on the paper roll (6), by means of a counter-pressure cylinder (7).

In the most recent version of this machine, the ink basin and rubber ink roller have been eliminated; their place is taken by a tube that feeds ink to the machine, and two wiper blades clean the screen cylinder. The remainder of the steps in the procedure are the same.

FROM THE TV STUDIO TO THE LIVING ROOM

Television is spectacular in two senses; on the one hand, it transmits spectacular images, and on the other hand, the way it works is spectacular, for it has the ability to place on a screen images received from radio waves.

The first president to appear on television (in black and white) was Franklin Delano Roosevelt, who participated in a demonstration at the 1939 New York World's Fair. After the demonstration, he stated, "Today

Filming for television is the same as filming for a movie, except that on TV the moving image can be broadcast as it happens. Filming a live performance requires perfect coordination from all the members of the crew—the journalists, camera and microphone operators, and the anchor.

In the control booth, the director must be a paragon of control, making instant decisions and choosing the best shots. There is no second chance when going out live.

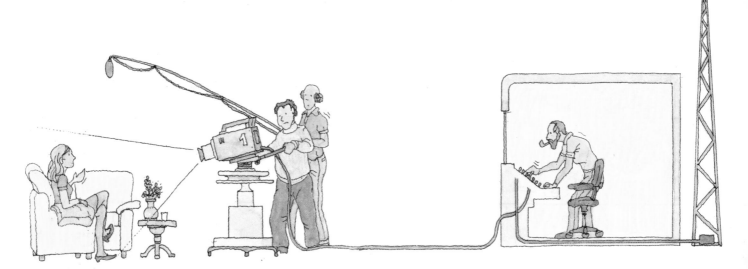

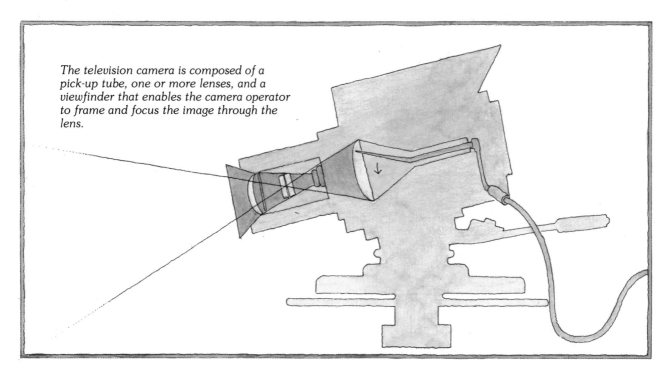

The television camera is composed of a pick-up tube, one or more lenses, and a viewfinder that enables the camera operator to frame and focus the image through the lens.

we have seen the future."

Television begins with a camera. A scene is shot, and the images captured by the camera lens are transformed into electrical signals, which create a continuous flow of current. This is amplified and sent into the atmosphere by an antenna that transmits high-frequency radio waves. The television receiver decodes these radio waves, rearranging the flow of current into electronic signals, which are projected onto the television screen by an electron gun, or "scanner." The main part of the television's system is the cathode-ray tube, where the flow of current is read and transformed into electrical signals, producing the images that we see on the screen.

The first TVs were very large and worked by thermionic tubes that took a long time to heat up. The evolution of television, however, has been remarkably rapid, marked by enormous leaps forward with developments in electronics (tran-

Do television viewers realize how much technology is behind that little screen? Only a few decades after the first black-and-white transmissions, we now have lifelike color images, hundreds of channels, public and private stations, and national and local broadcasts. We can even receive TV programs from across the world by erecting a dish antenna. We can see and hear what the pope or president says and witness events in distant lands immediately, just as they occur.

The images on the TV are electric signals projected on a screen of photoelectric material that transforms them into luminous dots. Television images make use of the physiological phenomenon of persistence of vision (an image is retained on the eye's retina so that a picture remains briefly visible after its actual disappearance). Television cameras scan the dots of images line by line, and the images are transmitted the same way, but with such rapidity that when the last dot in the last line is transmitted the viewer's retina is still seeing the first dot of the first line.

sistors and integrated circuits) and the passage from black and white to color.

Color television was made possible using the same processes already applied to color photography. Every color image can be broken down into the three primary colors, red, green, and blue, which can be combined to create all the other colors. The first stage in this process, color scanning, takes place in the color camera, where each image is transformed into three signals (one for each color); the second stage happens in the cathode-ray tube of the television, where the camera's electronic signals are recreated on the TV screen.

The cathode-ray tube is already becoming a thing of the past; new screens made of liquid crystals are wafer-thin and can be hung like pictures on a wall. They produce an image whose clarity reaches the limits of technological perfection.

Televisions are sometimes called "domestic appliances," but future developments promise to liberate the TV from the category of washing machines and refrigerators. The telecomputer is almost fully realized. This is an interactive TV, linked to a computer, so that people will be able to communicate, pay bills, go shopping, receive the entire contents of a library or a single page from a magazine or newspaper without leaving home.

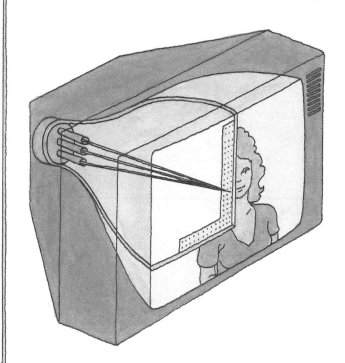

The best-known systems for producing color TV are the NTSC, which has been used in the United States since 1953; SECAM, used in France; and the PAL system, used in almost all the rest of Europe.

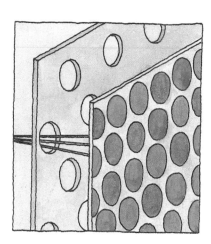

In the TV set, between the electron gun and the screen is a mosaic, which has thousands of openings through which the red, green, and blue signals pass to strike the screen. This mosaic is covered with tiny photoelectric cells that form the image.

TELEVISION: HOW THE PROGRAMS ARE MADE

Silence in the studio! The red lights on the cameras are glowing, the actors are saying their lines, the scene is being shot. Up in the control room, the director is watching the progress of the program and selecting the best shots on monitors, each of which is connected to a different camera in the studio. Seated next to the director are the audio mixer, who controls the music and sound for the program, and the video mixer. The studio assistant moves back and forth between the director and the crew and actors on the set.

This job is vital; he or she is responsible for everything that happens in the studio and must ensure that everything is in order.

Like making a movie, making a television program is a group endeavor in which each member of the team does his or her job in coordination with everyone else. This is why television studios are usually composed of people who enjoy their work and enjoy working together to find ways to improve their creations.

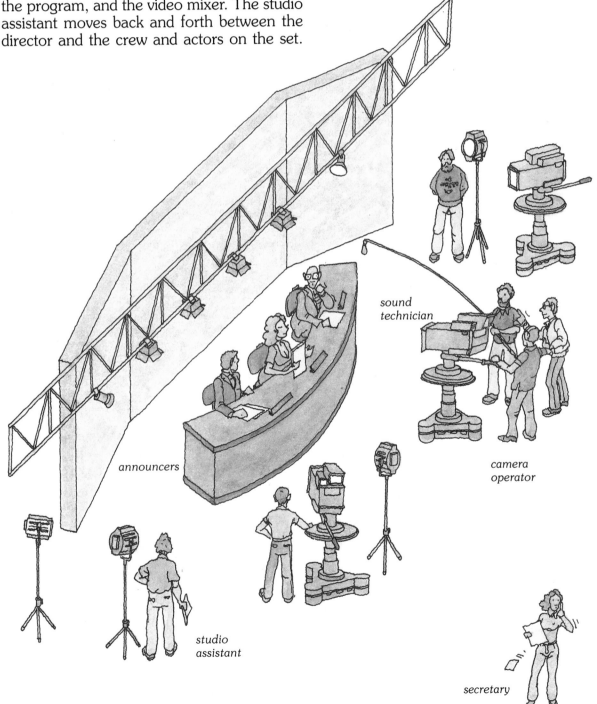

announcers

sound technician

camera operator

studio assistant

secretary

ADVERTISING

Advertisements: whatever you're doing, wherever you are, you can't fail to see them. You don't have to search for them; they're simply everywhere. This wasn't always the case, though. If you open a paper from sixty or seventy years ago, you will have to search to find one, probably at the foot of a page of type, in a ruled box hidden in acres of gray text. Street advertising was even scarcer: small metal signs above shops and posters or postcards, sometimes designed by famous artists like Henri Toulouse-Lautrec. Then, making use of all the new ways of communicating, advertisements suddenly began to expand, or explode, and they continue to do so today, when advertising is everywhere. Radio, for example, is an ideal means of advertising—the daytime drama programs we call soap operas got their name because they were once sponsored by soap manufacturers. Advertising has become television's best friend, to the extent that commercial TV stations could not exist without it.

What happened to make advertising

expand so much in so short a time? First, cities have grown into huge metropolises with enormous populations that advertisers can take advantage of by displaying ads on every available site all over town—neon signs, slogans, colored lights. And the means of communication that have made our world smaller have turned the world into a single marketplace. People are also wealthier and have new needs and desires, and even if they had no such desires to begin with, advertising has created them, simply by showing people what they do not have but can aspire to having.

Producing advertisements, however, is no easy matter. Huge numbers of people are involved, including artists, designers, psychologists, market researchers, copywriters, photographers, and printers. Every word, slogan, and image is carefully chosen, studied, and designed so it will have the most impact; every detail is analyzed. The ads must have the maximum impact and appear everywhere because after all that is their function—to be seen, to inspire dreams and promote desire.

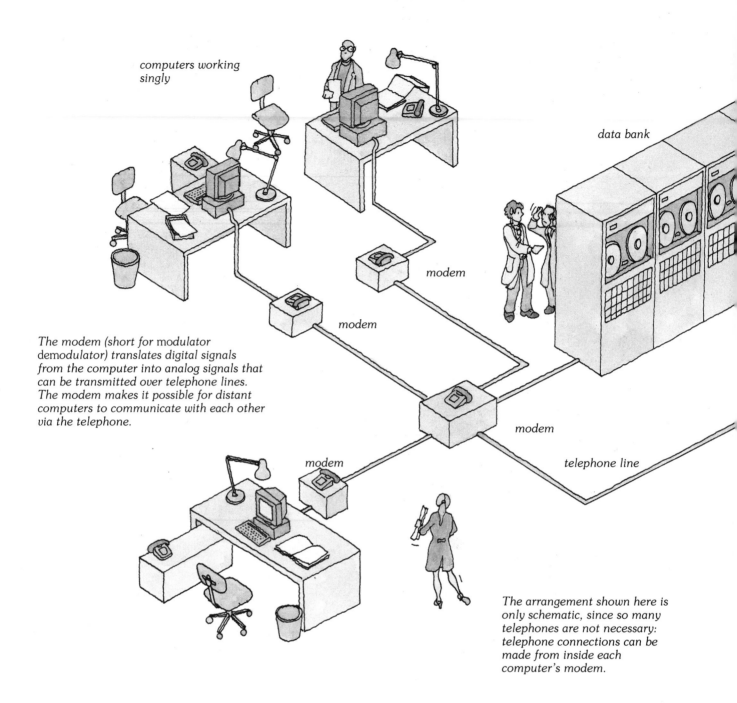

computers working singly

data bank

modem

modem

modem

The modem (short for modulator demodulator) translates digital signals from the computer into analog signals that can be transmitted over telephone lines. The modem makes it possible for distant computers to communicate with each other via the telephone.

modem

telephone line

The arrangement shown here is only schematic, since so many telephones are not necessary: telephone connections can be made from inside each computer's modem.

COMPUTER NETWORKS

"Hello, I am George."
"Hello, I am Massimo."
"I am calling from Australia."
"And I am answering from Italy."
"Pleased to meet you. I am a computer."
"So am I."

Computers can talk to each other. Any personal computer can be connected to others, creating an information network that works through the telephone lines and can be accessed by anyone with a telephone, a modem, a compatible computer, and the correct password. The possibilities are endless for exchanging information in this way, and in a few short years this technology has opened up many new and previously unforeseen uses. A computer can be connected to a data bank dealing with a specific subject matter—marketing, for instance, or statistics. Or it can be used in a more general way: someone at a home PC can initiate a dialogue, ask for information, and

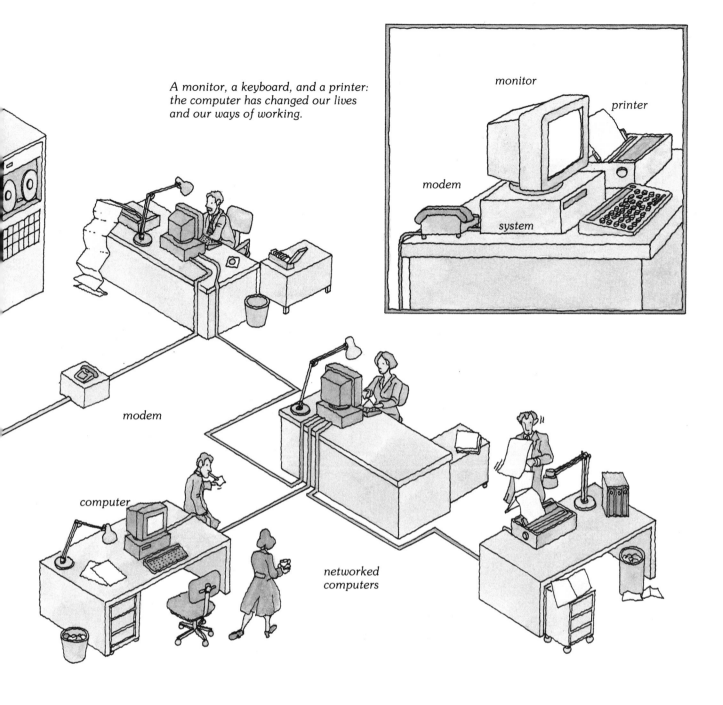

A monitor, a keyboard, and a printer: the computer has changed our lives and our ways of working.

modem

computer

modem

networked computers

monitor

printer

modem

system

at the same time put his or her own data at the disposal of other users in the network.

Like old-fashioned safes, the computer requires you to open a combination lock before it will reveal its contents. The computer's lock is known as a password, and once you are connected to the network, this word acts as the introduction or greeting. The computer will then recognize you as a friend and open the files you need. Once the dialogue is opened with the password, access is guaranteed.

SATELLITES

In ancient times, priests and sages scrutinized the skies and predicted the destiny of humankind according to the position of the stars and planets. Today, thousands of satellites travel across that same sky. Satellites are designed to perform many diverse, specific jobs. There are military and industrial research satellites, spy and intelligence satellites, satellites for meteorological data and satellites for intercontinental television and telephone connections. Satellites are particularly useful in communications; they can act as relays between transmitting and receiving stations on Earth.

They are also used to probe outer space beyond the confines of our planet, directing their antennas toward whatever might lie in the most distant and mysterious reaches of the universe—because the human desire to know and to communicate is never satisfied.

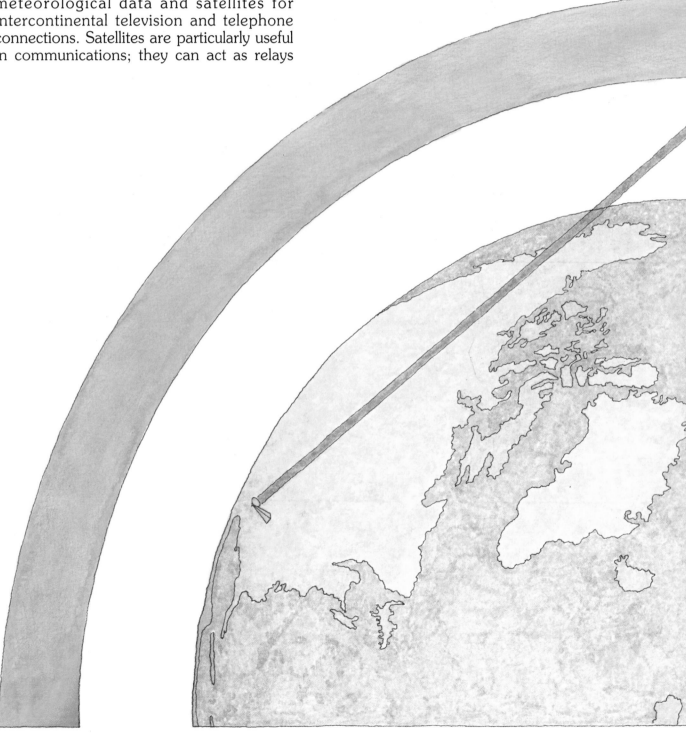

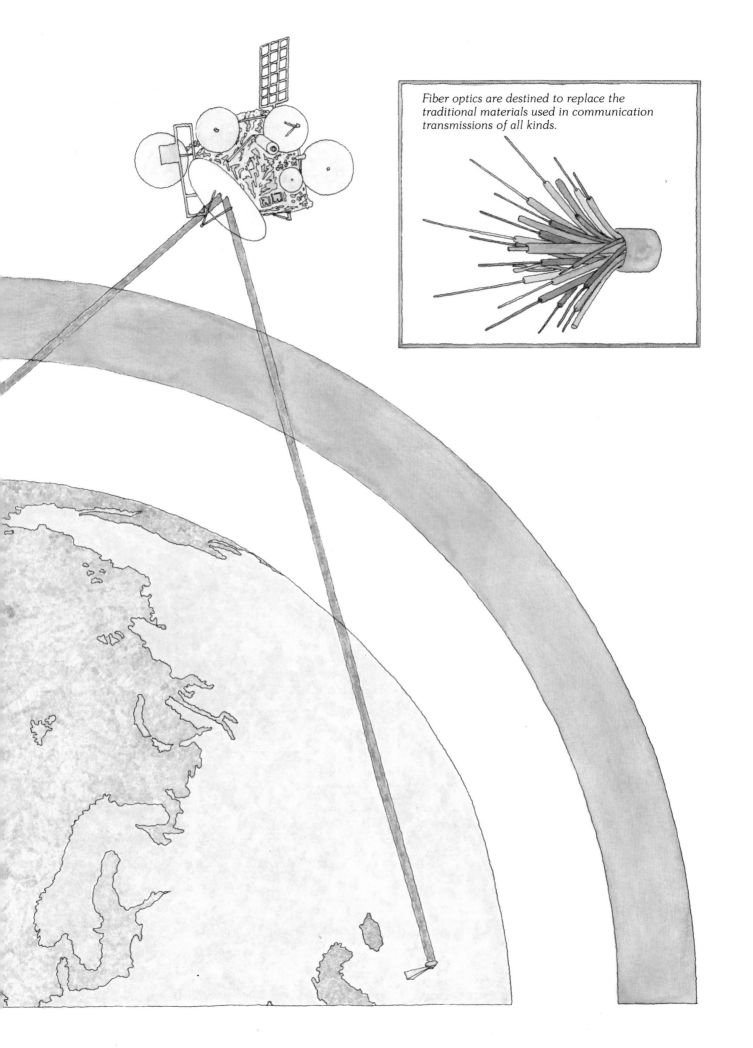

Fiber optics are destined to replace the traditional materials used in communication transmissions of all kinds.

GLOSSARY

Advertising The sponsored offering of goods or services through any medium of public communication; advertising informs potential consumers of the availability and quality of goods and services.

Aeschylus (525-456 B.C.). Greek tragic poet, one of the three fathers of Greek tragedy (with Sophocles and Euripides). He may have written as many as 90 plays, of which seven survive in full.

Alphabet Set of letters or other characters with which a language is written; the letters refer to the vocal sounds of the language, usually divided into vowels and consonants.

Antiphon A psalm, anthem, or verse from Scripture spoken or sung as part of the liturgy; their main use is in group singing of the Divine Office in a monastery. A book of antiphons is called an antiphonary.

Aristophanes (c. 448 B.C.-after 388 B.C.) Greek comic poet, known as the greatest ancient writer of comedy. Eleven of his plays survive.

Ballad Short, simple song in verse usually based on a popular legend or romance; ballads were once sung by traveling balladeers.

Bell, Alexander Graham (1847-1922) American scientist and inventor of the telephone.

Bible The sacred scriptures of Christians comprising the Old Testament and the New Testament. The Bible was the first book printed with movable type in the workshop of Gutenberg.

Charlie the Tramp Character invented by the celebrated actor and director Charlie Chaplin (1889-1977).

Cimabue (c. 1240-c. 1302) Florentine painter, whose real name was Cenni di Pepo, famous both for his paintings and also as the teacher of Giotto.

Coat of arms Insignia or emblems used to identify individuals and families during the Middle Ages; also known as armorial bearings, such emblems are used today for colleges, cities, and official government seals.

Codex Early form of book composed of manuscript pages folded and sewn together. The plural is codices.

Communication The transfer of thoughts and messages by various means, usually involving signs (sight) and sounds (hearing). Writing, painting, and television programs are forms of communication.

Computer An electronic device that can store, retrieve, and process information.

Coryphaeus The leader of a chorus in ancient Greek drama.

Daguerre, Louis Jacques Mandé (1789-1851) French inventor in 1839 of the daguerreotype, a photograph produced on a silver-coated copper plate treated with iodine vapor.

Dante Alighieri (1265-1321) Celebrated Florentine writer, author of the *Divine Comedy*, which recounts his imaginary journey through Hell, Purgatory, and Heaven. His other works include the *Convivio*, the *Rime*, and the *Vita Nuova*.

Diptych Two waxed tablets joined by a hinge so that they fold together to protect the writing on their waxed surfaces; used by the ancient Greeks and Romans, who wrote on wax tablets using a stylus.

Disney, Walt (1901-1966) Famous animator and film producer, creator of Mickey Mouse. Disney produced animated cartoons as long as standard movies, such as *Snow White and the Seven Dwarfs* and *Fantasia*.

Duccio di Buoninsegna (c. 1255-c. 1318). Italian painter celebrated for the *Rucellai Madonna*, painted in 1285.

Dummy A mock-up or model of a publication, such as a book or newspaper, that indicates the position of text and artwork for the printer.

Dürer, Albrecht (1471-1528) German painter and engraver, famous for splendid works that blend humanism, naturalism, and powerful creativity.

Edison, Thomas Alva (1847-1931) American inventor of the phonograph, incandescent lamp, carbon telephone transmitter, among many other inventions.

Engraving Art of cutting lines in metal, wood, or other material for reproduction through printing.

Epigraphy The art of writing on durable material, such as stone; the branch of archaeology devoted to the reading of such inscriptions is also known as epigraphy.

Etching Art of engraving with acid on a metal plate, usually copper or zinc.

Euripides (c. 480 or 485 B.C.-406 B.C.) Greek tragic poet, considered one of the fathers of Greek tragedy.

Fiber optics Thin, transparent, flexible rods of glass or plastic that transmit light by internal reflection and are used most of all in telecommunications.

Film A thin strip of flexible material coated with a light-sensitive emulsion on which photographic images are registered used to make photographs and motion pictures; also, a single motion picture.

Giotto (c. 1267-1337) Italian painter and architect who was a pupil of Cimabue. Among his famous frescoes are *The Life of St. Francis* and *St. John the Baptist*. In 1334 he planned and began construction of the belltower next to the cathedral in Florence.

Graffito Generic term for marks scratched on a surface (rock, ceramic, plaster, bone, metal, etc.); such marks can be decorations or inscriptions. The term *graffiti* is used by archaeologists for informal writings on tombs and ancient monuments.

Gutenberg, Johann (c. 1397-1468) German printer credited with being the first European to print with movable type. His most famous creation was a Bible.

Heraldry The study of armorial insignia, such as coats of arms.

Hertz, Heinrich Rudolf (1857-1894) German physicist who confirmed the electromagnetic theory of Maxwell and produced and studied electromagnetic waves (also known as hertzian waves or radio waves).

Hieroglyphs A system of writing using pictorial characters; the best-known hieroglyphs are those of the ancient Egyptians.

Hill, Rowland Inventor of the postage stamp. The first stamps were issued in England on May 6, 1840.

Ideogram A picture or symbol used in writing that does not represent a word or phrase but rather an idea or thing; numerals are an example of ideograms.

Illumination The decoration of manuscript books with gold or silver, elaborate designs, or the colored and gilded pictures known as miniatures.

Incunabula Name given to books printed in the 15th century, the oldest of which is the Bible printed by Gutenberg in 1453-55.

Information Knowledge, such as facts and data, obtained through communication. In the broadest sense, information is any facts or data communicated to a living being or machine.

Jongleurs Traveling entertainers of the Middle Ages who in addition to juggling and acrobatics also danced, performed magic tricks, sang, and told stories.

Legend A story from the past, usually based on a historical or religious subject, in which truth and fantasy are mixed. Like myths, legends were created and developed through oral traditions and were then later collected and written down.

Lithography Printing process in which the image to be printed is applied to a surface (such as smooth stone) using a lithographic crayon or ink that contains soap or grease; the areas of the image are thus ink-receptive while the blank areas are ink-repellent.

Lumière, Louis (1864-1948) and Auguste (1862-1954) French brothers who invented the first mechanism for photographing and projecting moving pictures on a screen.

Manuscript A text written by hand; also a handwritten book as distinguished from a printed book.

Manutius, Aldus (1450-1515) Venetian printer and editor who published editions of Greek and Roman classics and small-format books at low cost, the prototypes of the modern printed book.

Marconi, Guglielmo (1874-1937) Italian scientist and inventor celebrated for his development of the wireless telegraph. He received the Nobel Prize in Physics in 1909.

Martini, Simone (c. 1284-1344) Italian painter famous for his frescoes of the life of St. Martin, portrait of Guidoriccio da Fogliano, and *Annunciation*.

Maxwell, James Clerk (1831-1879) Scottish physicist who developed the theory of the electromagnetic field, a basic step in the development of the radio.

Meucci, Antonio (1808-1889) Italian inventor of the telephone. His legal dispute with Alexander Graham Bell was resolved by the Supreme Court, which acknowledged his invention.

Miniature In general terms, any small, detailed painting; in particular, a painting in an illuminated book or manuscript.

Minstrels Traveling entertainers of the Middle Ages who performed acrobatics as well as dancing and singing.

Modem A device that converts signals from one form to a form compatible with another kind of equipment (the name comes from *mo*dulator and *dem*odulator); modems are of importance in the field of telecommunications.

Morse, Samuel Finley (1791-1872) American inventor and artist, best known for his perfected version of the telegraph using a code composed of dots and dashes. He demonstrated the instrument's practicability in 1844 by sending a message over a wire from Washington to Baltimore.

Morse code Code used for transmitting messages by telegraph or with a lamp in signaling based on dots and dashes; on the telegraph the dots and dashes are indicated by the length of time the key is depressed.

Motion pictures General term for films—or movies—as an art and an industry, including production techniques, creative artists, and methods of distribution and displaying.

Movable type Method of printing that revolutionized the processes of reproducing writing. Movable type involves the arrangement of individual cast letters to form words and lines of text.

Newspaper Means of communication issued periodically and based on printing processes. Newspapers are made in varying formats (magazine, tabloid), are printed and distributed on varying schedules (daily, weekly, monthly), and can be devoted to topics of interest to particular groups of readers (such as fashion or financial newspapers).

Phonograph Device for reproducing sound that has been recorded as a spiral groove on a disk; the disk is known as a phonograph record, and phonographs are known as record players.

Photography The science and art of using various procedures to register permanent images on light-sensitive materials. As a tool for communication, photography can be considered as important as the printing press.

Pictographs A writing system based on symbolic or figurative symbols that are used to represent concepts.

Postal service The arrangements made by a government to meet the public need for communication between people by providing for the regular transmission of letters, packages, and periodicals.

Press A device used for printing and the establishment where matter is printed. In a broad sense, press refers to printed matter in general, particularly newspapers (weeklies, dailies, etc.), and their effect on public opinion (news, criticism, official communications).

Printing The art, process, and business of reproducing multiple copies of illustrations and words using a printing press or similar means.

Procession Religious ceremony in which a group of worshipers and church officials slowly walk along a street or inside a church accompanying a statue or sacred image while reciting prayers or singing hymns.

Radio Device for the wireless transmission and reception of electric impulses or signals—and thus information, performances, music—by means of electromagnetic waves; in a general sense the term also refers to the radio broadcasting industry.

Ravizza, Giuseppe Italian lawyer and inventor in 1837 of the writing cembalo, the first modern version of the typewriter.

Remington American manufacturer of weapons, agricultural implements, and sewing machines that in 1874 began making typewriters based on the patent of Sholes and Glidden.

Romulus and Remus Mythical founders of Rome; the twin sons of the god Mars and Rhea Silvia, they were set adrift in a basket on the Tiber and saved and raised by a she-wolf.

Roosevelt, Franklin Delano (1882-1945) President of the United States, elected three times (1933, 1936, and 1941).

Satellite Man-made object placed in orbit around the earth or other celestial body; most satellites are lifted from the earth's surface by rocket. Satellites serve many functions related to scientific research, military information, telecommunications, and meteorology.

Signal The sound or image transmitted by a telegraph, telephone, radio, radar, or television.

Sophocles (c. 496-406 B.C.) Greek tragic poet, one of the fathers of Greek tragedy, who wrote about 123 dramas.

Standard In ancient armies, such as that of the Romans, the standard was a pole bearing a banner or other highly visible object used to identify a unit and serve as a rallying point in battle.

Stele An upright stone or marble slab bearing inscriptions and decorations of a commemorative or funerary nature; the ancient Greeks and Romans used stelae as monuments or placed them in the walls of buildings.

Symbol Sign that stands for or suggests some universal or particular idea or value; for example, the hearth is a symbol of home.

Telegraph Device for long-distance communication using the electric transmission of signals in code over wire. The method in use throughout most of the world is based on the work of Samuel F. B. Morse and involves the reception of a series of impulses based on the Morse code. The term *telegraph* has also been applied to other methods of visible or audible signaling, such as smoke signals and drums.

Telephone Device for communicating sound, especially speech, by means of wires in an electrical circuit. The device transmits and receives signals.

Television Electronic system for the transmission and reception of images and sound. The term also refers to the television broadcasting industry and to the television receiving set itself.

Theater Place used for the performance of dramatic or musical works or spectacles of any kind; in general, theater refers to the dramatic works of a culture or civilization (such as Greek or Elizabethan theater).

Toulouse-Lautrec, Henri de (1864-1901) French painter and lithographer. He is most famous for his posters of dancers and personalities.

Troubadour Poet-musicians associated with the aristocracy of medieval Europe who wrote songs about courtly love, war, and nature. The term is also used for any strolling minstrel.

Typewriter A machine for writing in characters similar to printer's type operated by means of a keyboard and using letters that strike an inked ribbon. The first practical typewriter was invented by Christopher Latham Sholes and his associate Carlos Glidden and was manufactured by the Remington company beginning in 1874. Today the typewriter has been almost entirely replaced by computerized word-processing systems.

Typography The art of printing from movable type.

Wireless telegraph Telegraphy that uses radio waves without connecting wires. The term is also used as a synonym for radio.

Woodcut A print made from a design cut into a wooden block.

Writing The visible recording of language, writing is a type of communication fundamental to every people and all complex civilizations.